WHEN I GET BIGGER

BY MERCER MAYER

A GOLDEN BOOK • NEW YORK

Western Publishing Company, Inc., Racine, Wisconsin 53404

When I get bigger
I'll be able to do
lots of things.

I'll wait until the light is green. Then I'll look both ways for cars before I cross the street.

I'll have my own watch and I'll tell everyone what time it is.

I'll go on a bus
to Grandma and
Grandpa's.

When I get bigger I'll have
a real leather football ...

...my own radio, and a pair of
super-pro roller skates.

I'll have a two-wheeler and a paper route.
I'll make lots of money.

At the playground
I'll help the little kids
on the swings.

I'll pick out
my own boots
at the shoe store.

I'll make a phone call
and dial it myself.

I'll order something from a catalog...

...and it will come in the mail.

When I get bigger I'll camp out in the backyard all night long.

Or I'll stay up to
see the end of the
late movie.
Even if I get sleepy,
I won't go to bed.

But right now I have to go to bed…

...because Mom and Dad say...

...I'm not bigger yet.